SACRAMENTO PUBLIC LIBRARY
3 3029 05330 6940

D1006233

A Note to Parents and Teachers

Kids can imagine, kids can laugh and kids can learn to read with this exciting new series of first readers. Each book in the Kids Can Read series has been especially written, illustrated and designed for beginning readers. Humorous, easy-to-read stories, appealing characters, and engaging illustrations make for books that kids will want to read over and over again.

To make selecting a book easy for kids, parents and teachers, the Kids Can Read series offers three levels based on different reading abilities:

Level 1: Kids Can Start to Read

Short stories, simple sentences, easy vocabulary, lots of repetition and visual clues for kids just beginning to read.

Level 2: Kids Can Read with Help

Longer stories, varied sentences, increased vocabulary, some repetition and visual clues for kids who have some reading skills, but may need a little help.

Level 3: Kids Can Read Alone

Longer, more complex stories and sentences, more challenging vocabulary, language play, minimal repetition and visual clues for kids who are reading by themselves.

With the Kids Can Read series, kids can enter a new and exciting world of reading!

Sam's First Halloween

Written by Mary Labatt

Illustrated by Marisol Sarrazin

Kids Can Press

Kids Can Press acknowledges the financial support of the Ontario Arts Council, the Canada Council for the Arts and the Government of Canada, through the BPIDP, for our publishing activity.

Published in Canada by
Kids Can Press Ltd.
29 Birch Avenue
Toronto, ON M4V 1E2

Published in the U.S. by
Kids Can Press Ltd.
2250 Military Road
Tonawanda, NY 14150

www.kidscanpress.com

Edited by David MacDonald
Designed by Stacie Bowes and Marie Bartholomew
Printed in Hong Kong, China

The hardcover edition of this book is smyth sewn casebound.
The paperback edition of this book is limp sewn with a drawn-on cover.

CM 03 0 9 8 7 6 5 4 3 2 1
CM PA 03 0 9 8 7 6 5 4 3 2 1

National Library of Canada Cataloguing in Publication Data

Labatt, Mary, date.
Sam's first Halloween / written by Mary Labatt ; illustrated by Marisol Sarrazin.

(Kids can read)
ISBN 1-55337-355-3 (bound). ISBN 1-55337-356-1 (pbk.)

I. Sarrazin, Marisol, 1965- II. Title. III. Series: Kids can read (Toronto, Ont.)

PS8573.A135S25 2003 jC813'.54 C2002-904610-6 PZ7

Kids Can Press is a Corus™ Entertainment company

Joan and Bob had something orange.

"It is a pumpkin

for Halloween," said Bob.

Joan made a face

on the pumpkin.

Bob put candy in a dish.

"Hmmm," thought Sam.

"What is Halloween?"

The doorbell rang.

A ghost was at the door.

"Trick or treat," said the ghost.

Joan got the candy dish.

"This is good," thought Sam.

"I like candy."

Joan gave candy to the ghost.

“What about me?”

thought Sam.

"Woof!" said Sam.

She sniffed the candy dish.

Joan did not give candy to Sam.

A vampire and a robot

came to the door.

A ladybug came, too.

"Trick or treat," they said.

Sam sat next to Bob.

"Woof!" she said.

Bob did not give candy to Sam.

A fairy and a monster

came to the door.

"Trick or treat," they said.

Sam stuck her nose

in the candy bags.

"No, no, no!" said Joan.

Joan gave candy

to the fairy and the monster.

No one gave candy to Sam.

Sam jumped at the candy dish.

"Woof!" she said. "Woof! Woof!"

Bob did not look at Sam.

Sam flopped on the floor.

"The kids are having Halloween.

I want Halloween, too!"

The doorbell rang.

A witch and a lion

were at the door.

"Trick or treat," they said.

Joan gave candy

to the witch and the lion.

"This is bad," thought Sam.

"The kids are getting all the candy."

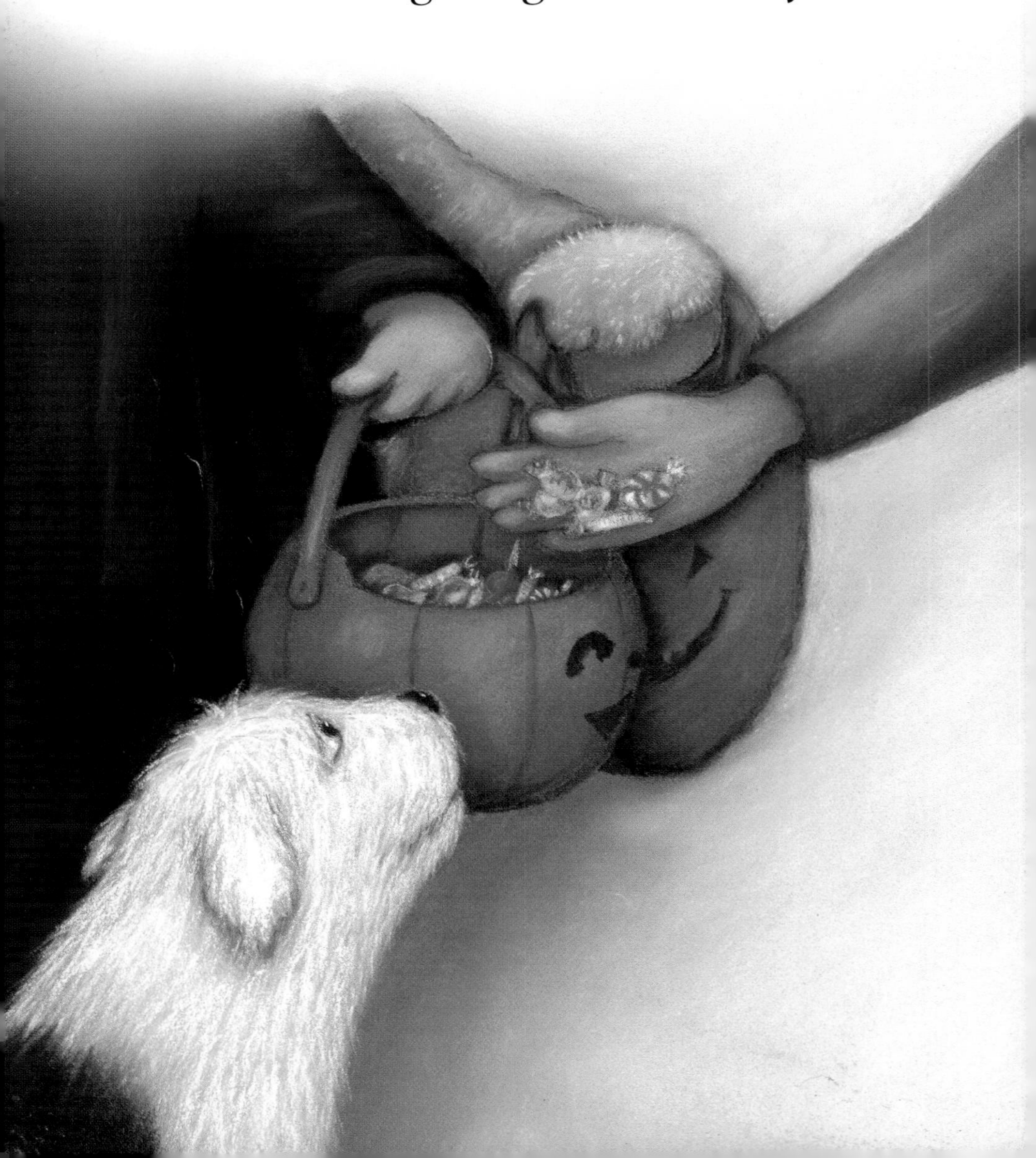

"Grrr," said Sam.

She jumped at the candy dish.

"I want Halloween!" she thought.

"I need candy!"

Sam looked up at the candy.

"I know how to get candy!

I can dress up like the kids,"

she thought.

Sam ran up to the bathroom.

She bit a towel and pulled.

"Good," thought Sam.

"I am a ghost.

Now I will get candy!"

The doorbell rang.

Sam ran down to the door.

“Here comes a ghost,” she thought.

“And the ghost needs candy!”

A princess and a pirate

were at the door.

A tiger came, too.

"Trick or treat," they said.

Sam ran fast.

She hid next to the princess.

Joan gave candy to the kids.

Sam jumped out.

"Woof!" she said.

"I am a ghost," she thought.

"And ghosts need candy!"

"Sam!" said Bob.

"What are you doing?" asked Joan.

"She wants candy!" said the tiger.

"Woof!" said Sam. "Woof! Woof!"

Joan and Bob laughed.

The princess and the pirate laughed.

The tiger laughed, too.

"What's so funny?" thought Sam.

"I need candy!"

"Candy is not for puppies," said Bob.

"Candy is for kids," said Joan.

Sam flopped down.

"Puppies need candy, too!" she thought.

The princess said, “Poor puppy.”

The tiger said, “Poor, poor puppy.”

The pirate said, “She can have my candy.”

Joan and Bob looked at each other.

Joan said, “Well, maybe she can have one.”

The pirate gave Sam a candy.

"YUM! YUM!" thought Sam.

"I like Halloween!"

"Let's have Halloween every day!"